The Ugly Duckling

Retold Story of The Ugly Duckling

By Marla Tomlinson

Fables and Folktales
Prefixes and Suffixes

Scan this code to access the Teacher's Notes for this series or visit
www.norwoodhousepress.com/decodables

NORWOOD HOUSE PRESS

DEAR CAREGIVER, *The Decodables* series contains books following a systematic, cumulative phonics scope and sequence aligned with the science of reading. Each book allows its reader to apply their phonics knowledge in engaging and relatable texts. The words within each text have been carefully selected to ensure that readers can rely on their decoding skills as they encounter new or unfamiliar words. They also include high frequency words appropriate for the target skill level of the reader.

When reading these books with your child, encourage them to sound out words that are unfamiliar by attending to the target letter(s) and sounds. If the unknown word is an irregularly spelled high frequency word or a word containing a pattern that has yet to be taught (challenge words) you may encourage your child to attend to the known parts of the word and provide the pronunciation of the unknown part(s). Rereading the texts multiple times will allow your child the opportunity to build their reading fluency, a skill necessary for proficient comprehension.

You can be confident you are providing your child with opportunities to build their decoding abilities which will encourage their independence as they become lifelong readers.

Happy Reading!

Emily Nudds, M.S. Ed Literacy
Literacy Consultant

Norwood House Press • www.norwoodhousepress.com
The Decodables ©2024 by Norwood House Press. All Rights Reserved.
Printed in the United States of America.

Library of Congress Cataloging-in-Publication Data has been filed and is available at https://lccn.loc.gov/2023018583

Literacy Consultant: Emily Nudds, M.S.Ed Literacy
Editorial and Production Development and Management: Focus Strategic Communications Inc.
Editors: Christine Gaba, Christi Davis-Martell
Illustration Credit: Mindmax

Hardcover ISBN: 978-1-68450-674-3   Paperback ISBN: 978-1-68404-917-2
eBook ISBN: 978-1-68404-971-4

It was spring. The mother duck sat on her nest. She was waiting. She was seated on top of four eggs she had laid.

Three were the same size. One was larger than the rest. She was unsure why it was bigger. But she hoped they would all be adorable ducklings.

One day, the ducklings hatched. Three were adorable. They were golden and very handsome. The other duckling was gray. He was bigger than the others and not nearly as cute.

"What is this?" the mother duck asked. "Why is this baby so gray?"

The other ducks laughed. The gray duckling felt unhappy.

5

The ducks started to grow. The three golden ducks were mean to the gray one. They said unkind things.

"Look at his feathers," they said. "They are dirty. And he is so big. He is the largest duck we have ever seen!"

They would sneak up on him and scare him.

"Boo!" They found it funny when he jumped.

The gray duckling was very careful to **avoid** them.

The gray duck was very unhappy.

He felt unwanted by his siblings.

"I will go seek a new place to live," he said. "I will find other ducks who do not dislike me. I will make my way to a new home in the morning."

The gray duck had a sleepless night. He was unable to sleep because he was worried about leaving.

"I am mistreated here," he said. "The others dislike me so I will find a family with kindness who will take me in."

He knew he had to go. He continued on his journey.

The gray duck had walked for a long time when he saw an **odd** thing. A rabbit, mouse, and squirrel were having a picnic.

It was midday and the gray duck felt very hungry.

"Hello," said the gray duck in a tiny voice. "May I join you?"

"Who are you?" asked the rabbit.

"I am a duck," said the gray duck.

"You are a duck?" asked the rabbit. "You look dirty and you do not look like a duck."

The rabbit laughed and the others joined him.
The rabbit seemed to be the leader.

"If I were you," he said in an impolite voice,
"I would disappear!"

The mouse smiled and threw a berry at him.
"Now you are messy!" The squirrel laughed.

"You are childish," yelled the gray duck. He did
not like this nonsense, so he left.

13

The gray duck walked all summer. It seemed endless.

He tried to befriend many animals, but they were all unkind.

"I don't get it! What is wrong with being gray? I am a big gray duck. How does this make me **unworthy** of basic kindness? This is unfair!"

He started to cry.

And as he cried, the leaves started to fall.

Time passed. It was getting colder and started snowing.

The gray duck had nowhere to go and was becoming fearful. "It is too cold now!"

He was shivering and upset, so he hid under a bush and fell asleep.

He was woken about an hour later when he felt himself being lifted off the ground. A farmer had found the gray duck and was carrying him under his arm.

"Let's get you home and unfreeze you," said the farmer kindly.

The farmer lived in a little house near the lake. He used a big old key to unlock his door. Inside was an untidy home with an overstuffed armchair by a fireplace. The fire was roaring, and in front of it was a cat and a hen.

They looked at the farmer and duck sleepily. The gray duck felt uneasy. He knew what was coming and he was filled with sadness.

18

"What strange bird is that?" asked the cat.

"Yuck," said the hen.

The unhappy duck thought he should leave. But it was too cold outside, so he stayed.

Spring finally came. The sun melted the snow. The grass appeared.

The gray duck felt hopeful.

He knew the goodness of the farmer, but the cat and hen were awful.

He left the house and headed toward the lake. When he got there, his heart sank. There were many large white birds in the lake swimming.

"Who are you?" the largest bird asked.

"I am a gray duck," he said **timidly**.

"I do not think you are a gray duck. You may have been gray when you were a baby, but now your feathers are white."

The gray duck felt uncertain. He was feeling less gray.

"It is not believable that you are a duck. Ducks are not white. And your neck is much longer."

The sadness in the gray duck started again. This new bird might be mean like the others.

The bird said, "You, my graceful friend, are one of us. You are a swan. Look at your reflection in the water!"

The gray duck looked. And he saw that what others had said before was untrue. He was not an unclean gray duck. He had grown to be a lovely swan!

The white swan swam out to the others and began to play happily.

Glossary

avoid: keep away from

odd: unusual

timidly: fearfully

unworthy: do not deserve

Prefixes and Suffixes

Prefixes

asleep	mistreated	overstuffed	unkind	untrue
disappear	nonsense	uncertain	unsure	unworthy
dislike	nowhere	uneasy	untidy	upset
impolite				

Suffixes

adorable	continued	hopeful	roaring	started
asked	endless	largest	sadness	stayed
awful	fearful	leader	seated	timidly
bigger	golden	leaving	shivering	toward
careful	graceful	longer	sleepily	walked
carrying	happily	lovely	sleepless	woken
childish	having	melted	smiled	worried
colder	headed	passed	snowing	

High-Frequency Words

animals	found	large	new	very
because	here	live	should	walked
does	kindness	mother	unwanted	

Challenging Words

befriend	believable	laughed	strange